An Eyeball in My Garden

And Other Spine-Tingling Poems

Selected and edited by
Jennifer Cole Judd

and

Laura Wynkoop

with illustrations by
Johan Olander

MARSHALL CAVENDISH CHILDREN

Web site: www.marshallcavendish.us/kids

Other Marshall Cavendish Offices:
Marshall Cavendish International (Asia) Private Limited, 1 New Industrial Road, Singapore 536196 • Marshall Cavendish International (Thailand) Co Ltd. 253 Asoke, 12th Flr, Sukhumvit 21 Road, Klongtoey Nua, Wattana, Bangkok 10110, Thailand • Marshall Cavendish (Malaysia) Sdn Bhd, Times Subang, Lot 46, Subang Hi-Tech Industrial Park, Batu Tiga, 40000 Shah Alam, Selangor Darul Ehsan, Malaysia

Marshall Cavendish is a trademark of Times Publishing Limited

Library of Congress Cataloging-in-Publication Data
An eyeball in my garden : and other spine-tingling poems / selected and edited by Jennifer Cole Judd and Laura Wynkoop ; with illustrations by Johan Olander. — 1st ed.
p. cm.
ISBN 978-0-7614-5655-1
1. Fear—Juvenile poetry. 2. Supernatural—Juvenile poetry. 3. Monsters—Juvenile poetry. 4. Ghosts—Juvenile poetry. 5. Halloween—Juvenile poetry. 6. Horror—Juvenile poetry. 7. Children's poetry, American. 8. Humorous poetry, American. I. Judd, Jennifer Cole. II. Wynkoop, Laura. III. Olander, Johan, ill.
PS595.S94E94 2010   808.81'937—dc22   2010008081

The illustrations were rendered in ink on paper and enhanced in Adobe Photoshop.

Book design by Vera Soki

Printed in China (E)
First edition
1 3 5 6 4 2

To Bill and The Poets' Garage,
whose talents and support brought this book to life
—J.C.J. and L.W.

For Olivia and Vivienne
—J.O.

Contents

Spooky

By M. Sullivan

He's darkest night
On the darkest street.
The haunting shuffle
Of a stranger's feet.

He's the gnarled tree
And its grasping vine.
The icy finger
Down your tingling spine.

He's the shifting form
In a swirling fog.
The glowing eyes
Of the stalking dog.

He's the wrenching creak
Beneath your floors
As you dash inside
And bolt the doors.

He's the fear
That seeps into your bones
When there's silence
On your telephone.

He'll find you when
You're all alone.

He's Spooky.

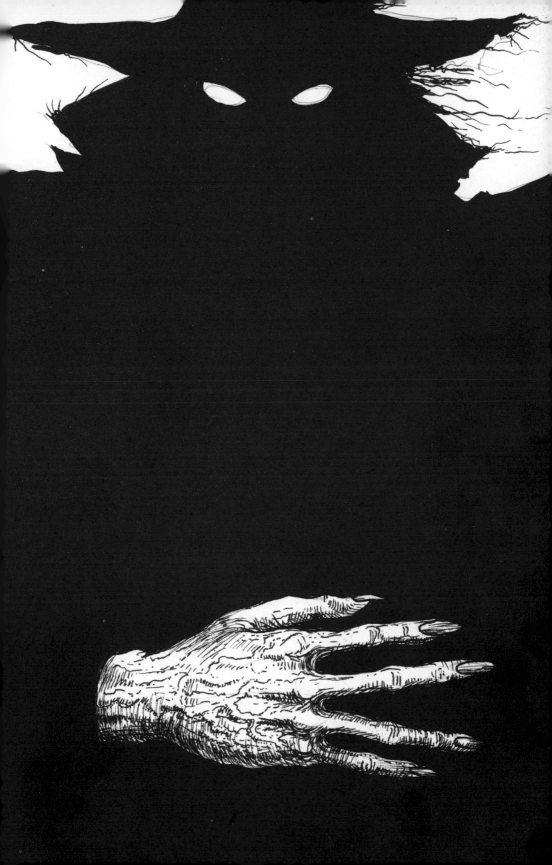

Bat

By Jennifer Cole Judd

Night worker
    Swiftly swoops—
        Shaving shreds of sky
            With razor wings.

        Night hunter
      Deftly dives—
    Searching silent fields
For creeping things.

Sleepy Spider

By Sue Davidson

Skinny legs, they dingle, dangle,
Weaving shadows at an angle.
Hairy legs so softly creeping,
Tippy-toeing as you're sleeping.
On the pillow, near your head,
Sleepy spider goes to bed.

Hixon House

By Susie Sawyer

Down a dark, dusty road on Halloween night,
The Hixon House anxiously waits.
It watches from windows, so long ago shattered,
And peers through its black iron gates.

Like unruly hair, its ramshackle roof
Wears a wandering, rambling vine.
Its creaky door gapes like a sad, crooked mouth,
Emitting a pitiful whine.

At last, around midnight, a thrill-seeking soul
Sets his lingering worries aside.
With flashlight in hand and eager heart pounding,
The visitor tiptoes inside.

He sneaks through the halls and climbs up the stairs,
Exploring the house from within.
Then doors slam around him and locks fasten tight,
And terror crawls over his skin.

From deep in its belly, the Hixon House rumbles
A curse, and the boy turns to stone.
His panicked expression preserved for all time;
Now the house is no longer alone.

Halloween Night

By Laura Wynkoop

After trick-or-treating's done,
And you fall fast asleep,
The decorations in your yard
Awake and start to creep.

Rubber spiders on their webs
Pursue their prey with ease,
As dangling ghosts untie their strings
To float among the trees.

Jack-o'-lanterns whisper tales
Of knives and pumpkin pie,
While fabric bats unfold their wings
And flitter through the sky.

Tattered witches mount their brooms
To race above the streets,
As Dracula steps off the porch
In search of tasty treats.

Now if you find it frightening
That all these creatures creep,
Rest assured; you'll be just fine
As long as you're asleep.

Sinking Ship

By M. Sullivan

Silent was the water as it rose above me head.
Poor unsuspectin' crew, they never made it out of bed.
Through a port I slid meself before the ship went down.
Oh no, there's not another death that equals bein' drowned!
Killed by Mother Ocean, off the distant Spanish coast—
'Tis good ya can't die more than once. . . . I's already a ghost.

Bedtime Story

By Susie Sawyer

"Please tell me the story," the little one said.
"All right," whispered Grandma, "but then, off to bed.
      I lived my whole life in this house, as you know,
      But someone else joined me a few months ago.
      At first I heard voices and noises downstairs,
      Then furniture moving, like tables and chairs.
      I think there are four of them; two are quite small.
      They roam about freely and pass through the hall.
      When I am awake, they make scarcely a peep,
      But they cause such a racket when I go to sleep!
      I've asked them to leave, yet they don't seem to hear.
      It's almost as if they can't see me, my dear.
      So I have decided to just let them be;
      I stay clear of them, and they stay clear of me.
      Now, if you should happen to see one someday,
      Do not be afraid and do not run away.
      Just mind your own business and don't make a fuss.
      They're harmless and not all that different from us.
Remember, my dear, Grandma loves you the most.
Now head off to bed. Be a good little ghost."

Where Nightmares Dwell

By Craig W. Steele

Not far away,
A forest dwells
In darkness, overgrown
With snaking brambles, brooding trees,
As werewolves howl and spirits moan.

And every night,
At midnight's stroke,
The bat-faced shadows creep
From pitch-black caves to steal the dreams
Of precious children fast asleep.

They wriggle deep
Into your mind,
And light your darkest fears,
Then drag you down to nightmare land,
A place of haunting screams and tears.

I know too well
What creatures lurk
Where nightmares live and grow.
I go there every night, dear child—
The shadows found me years ago!

Camp Creepy

By Craig W. Steele

We're gathered 'round the campfire's flames
For ghostly tales and spooky games.
Our shrieking rings throughout the hills—
Those haunting echoes give me chills.

Far out beyond the campfire's light,
The wind cries *Ooohh!* as if in fright,
And owls hoot softly while they fly
Across the gloomy, moonless sky.

As grumbling thunder shakes the ground,
The shadow fires dance around.
They flicker through the swaying trees,
While bushes rustle in the breeze.

I see dark creatures, left and right—
Three monsters circling in the night.
Their pinpoint eyes glow neon-red;
I'm certain we will soon be dead.

A log explodes with blazing CRACKS!
I scream and jump and spill my snacks.
Then suddenly I realize
There are no glaring monster eyes.

I was just dreaming, all is well.
I yawn and stretch . . . then gasp and yell,
For things are worse than I had feared—
All my friends have disappeared!

Rise and Shine

By William Shakespeery

Behind a house at noon today,
I woke from being dead,
And burrowed out from underneath
My neighbor's flowerbed.
I brushed the earth and beetles off,
Then tried to be polite.
"How do you do?" I greeted her,
But she turned ghostly white.
"Oh, please excuse the worm," I said,
"That's diggin' in my eye.
I sure could use a little drink;
My throat is gravely dry."
Just then I sneezed; my neighbor screamed
And leapt into the air.
"Don't run," I hollered. "Please come back.
My nose is in your hair!"

My Date with Mummy

By Jennifer Cole Judd

I've burned the scones and muffins,
And brewed my blackest tea.
Everything must be just right
For Mummy's date with me.

I've draped the lamps with cobwebs,
Placed flowers on the sill.
The finest roses, dead and dried,
Will give her such a thrill.

I splash on my new aftershave—
It's Eau de Ninety-Volts.
My suit is tight, it fits just right,
It sets off my new bolts.

She's waiting on the porch step.
Her wraps look so divine!
I kiss her hand, and Mummy smiles.
"Why thank you, Frankenstein!"

Dracula Goes Coffin Shopping

By Laura Wynkoop

Dracula woke in his coffin one evening
And stretched as he opened the top.
His muscles were cramped, and his joints—how they ached—
He wanted the throbbing to stop!

"I'm sick of this old wooden box!" he exclaimed.
"It's time that I found a new bed.
Perhaps one with lining of velvet or silk,
And a pillow to cushion my head."

So Dracula dressed in his best three-piece suit
And limped to the funeral home.
He looked at the coffins in maple and walnut,
And copper and silver and chrome.

He opened each one and examined the hinges.
He studied each hand-carved design,
Then spotted a lining of blood-colored velvet
Inside a large coffin of pine.

"This coffin is perfect," the vampire announced.
"So luxurious, roomy, and deep!"
He lay down inside it and fluffed up the pillow,
Then Dracula fell fast asleep.

Just then the mortician appeared in the parlor
And gasped as he surveyed the room.
He knew that to wake this particular client
Would bring undeniable doom.

He called his assistant to write up the bill.
"Be careful! Don't wake him!" he cried.
Then they loaded the hearse and delivered the coffin
With Dracula sleeping inside!

Come Closer, Closer. . . .

By Shirley Anne Ramaley

So still, I'm waiting.
Come closer, my dear.
You don't see my web,
But I'm over here.

Do you feel afraid?
You've nothing to fear.
Keep flying this way
Until you are near.

Did you say your prayers?
Well, I'm praying, too.
But what you don't know is
I'm preying for you.

Come closer, closer. . . .

Full Moon

By Laura Wynkoop

O shining eye up in the sky,
You watch as darkness slithers by.
You beckon creatures, fierce and foul,
To stalk the shadowed hills and howl.
You know where all the witches dwell,
Who watch you as they weave each spell.
You turn a man into a beast
Upon your rising in the east.
You stir the spirits from their sleep,
Who whisper secrets old and deep.
O shining eye up in the sky,
For you, the darkness slithers by.

Witch's Shopping List

By Laura Wynkoop

Stinging nettles
Mandrake root
Stomach of a spotted newt
Powdered wolfsbane
Lace-wing flies
Forty spiny spider eyes
Alder broomstick
Mugwort tea
Berries from a hawthorn tree
Copper cauldron
Dragon horn
Silver hair of unicorn
Salamanders
Ginger juice
Needles of a weeping spruce
Wart remover
New black cat
(Since my last one's
now a rat)

Mummy's Menu

By Stella Michel

Fruit bat wings with hollandaise,
Eyeballs in a demi-glaze,
Cut-up wilted ragwort greens,
A side of wormy, wiggly beans,
Kidney stew with chunks of spine,
Pickled brains in zesty brine,
Roasted rat served over rice,
Scrumptious maggot-covered mice,
Blackened pudding filled with flies,
Crispy scarab beetle pies,
Ladyfingers, with the rings
(Mummies love those dainty things).
But what a shame! Oh, what a waste!
If only I could have a taste.
All the dishes sound so yummy.
Alas! This mummy has no tummy.

Winking Wot Warning

By Debra Leith

Have you ever met a Winking Wot?
They're warty and hairy and wink a lot.
They laugh and giggle, joke and cheer,
Wiggle and waggle each curly ear.

Like round, ripe lemons, their eyes are yellow;
A Winking Wot is the strangest fellow.
But when he stops winking, his eyes turn green;
He flips like a switch from nice to mean!

The Wots I've seen are three feet high,
With pointed feet turned toward the sky.
They teeter and totter on their heels;
They can't run fast to catch their meals.

But I've never seen a starving Wot,
And like bees drawn to a honey pot,
They lure their prey with waggles and cheers;
They laugh and joke until it nears.

So if you meet a Winking Wot
That's warty and hairy and winks a lot,
Check his eyes, 'cause if they're yellow,
The Wot will be an agreeable fellow.

But should you see his eyes turn green,
Beware! He'll be a fearsome fiend.
A Wot will laugh and joke and cheer,
Then gobble you up if you are near!

Graveyard Hill

By William Shakespeery

Errk, eeek, a fat rat squeaks,
A one-eyed stray cat yowls.
The willow groans and shakes its bones,
As Autumn's north wind howls.

Errk, eeek, a shadow shrieks,
While vampire bats take flight.
A raven squawks as Darkness walks,
And pairs of eyes ignite.

Errk, eeek, a coffin creaks,
The rows of tombstones quake.
There's nothing still on Graveyard Hill
When dead men start to wake.

Beneath the Stairs
By Stella Michel

Beneath the stairs where shadows creep,
Where spiders crawl and nightmares sleep,
The boogeyman's red, glowing eyes
Inspect the darkness for some prize—
A zesty bat, a yummy rat.
If he's in luck, a scrumptious cat.

The boogeyman adores fresh meat,
Things that scratch with skittery feet.
Writhing and thrashing inside his jaw,
He grinds them up and gulps them raw.

When dinner's through,
dessert is due.
And so he hides and
waits for you.

The Corner

By M. Sullivan

In the corner of your room awaits

A Shape.

A No-Shape.

A hint of eyes.

A dark you cannot see into.

You pick up a ball,
A book,
A doll,
Anything.

Into the corner it flies
but does not land.

Brave,
Curious,
Foolish,

You approach

And

Step

In.

In the corner of your room awaits

A Shape.

A No-Shape.

A hint of eyes.

A dark you cannot see out of.

Ghoul Song
By Sue Davidson

Let's growl and groan,
Let's crack some bones!
The ghouly season's here.
It's time to rise up from our graves
And fill the world with fear.

Our spirits speak,
We howl and shriek,
Our ghoulish choir is singing.
Sounds of darkness wake the dead
With all our voices ringing.

We're grim and gaunt,
We love to haunt,
We slither through the night.
So bite your nails, lock your doors,
And hug your pillows tight!

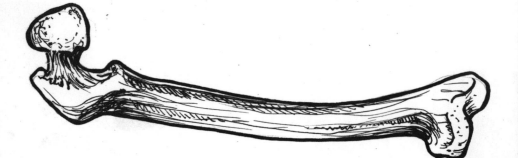

Zombie Kid Blues

By Edna Cabcabin Moran

Being a zombie is cool,
And normally I like school.
But today's not my day,
I'm sorry to say,
I'm falling apart like a fool.

While playing baseball outside,
I ended up wanting to hide.
Though I borrowed a mitt
That perfectly fit,
It came off with my hand still inside.

At lunch, we lined up at the door,
Where I was embarrassed once more.
I caused some alarm
When I lifted my arm,
Which fell off and rolled onto the floor.

I hope to be stitched up by dawn.
My worries will then be all gone.
Though I'll leave them behind,
I won't lose my mind
As long as my head stays on!

An Eyeball in My Garden

By William Shakespeery

Oh dear, oh dear, oh double dear!
It simply cannot be!
Between my roses there's an eyeball
Staring up at me.

What do I do, what *can* I do?
An eyeball's in my garden.
Will it stink and shrink away,
Or will it sit and harden?

And what if Kitty brings it in?
It might attract the ants.
I guess I could just flip it out
Into my neighbor's plants.

Oh dear, oh dear, oh double dear!
Oh, things are not so fine.
I scooped it up and realized
That lonely eyeball's mine!

Mad Scientist

By Christy Critchfield

We are excited for Halloween night,
Both dressed in our spooky attire.
I am a mummy wrapped tightly in white,
And my brother's a thirsty vampire.

We walk down the block and see Bad Brian Fist,
The big bully who ruins our fun.
He wears the disguise of a Mad Scientist
With a shiny new Shrinking Ray-Gun.

We scream and run fast, like a speeding torpedo,
But are hit with a strange shrinking vapor.
So now my poor brother's a tiny mosquito,
And I'm nothing but old toilet paper.

Igor Picks a Pet

By Stella Michel

No purry cat,
Or waggy dog.
I thinks me wants
This poison frog.

Or how 'bouts that
Electric ray?
Spine-tinglish fiend,
The witches say.

Perchance a gryphon
With knifesome claws?
A werewolf pup
With snappish jaws?

The vampire bat
With flapsy wings?
The red-eyed rat
Who chews dead things?

That fearsome viper
With fangs so bold?
Let's see—oh, no!
I haves no gold.

No flamey dragon
So scalesome cute—
Guess I'll just takes
This free dead newt.

39

Ghost Fish

By William Shakespeery

The goldfish had died an unfortunate death,
Now his ghost haunts the toilet at night.
Upside-down in the water,
He waits in the darkness,
His scales glowing skeleton-white.

"I won't be forgotten," he bubbles in silence,
While floating in fiendish delight.
And when sleepy-eyed people
Come park on the potty,
He leaps up and gives them a fright.

40

Voices

By Jennifer Cole Judd

A murmur down the hallway,
A wail upon the breeze.
A rustle from the patio,
A whisper in the trees.

A sigh inside my closet,
Behind my bed, a groan.
Why must these ghosts get chatty
Whenever I'm alone?

Owl

By Laura Wynkoop

A shadow lurks among the leaves,
Its amber eyes aglow.
As still as stone, it guards the night
Until it's summoned into flight.
With spectral wings, it rides the wind
To prey on those below.

Our Neighborhood

By Kevin McNamee

Welcome to our neighborhood
Where frightful things are seen,
When you go trick-or-treating
Down our street on Halloween.

We've candy from the dollar store,
At five bags for a buck.
That's what it cost ten years ago.
I think it's moving—*yuck!*

Ms. Johnson saves her pennies,
Which she gives out as a treat.
I think she stores them in her shoes—
Her pennies smell like feet!

The dentist hands out dental floss,
But never any sweets.
And crazy Mr. Haggerty
Gives grocery receipts.

Ms. Meyers wears a costume,
Which we think is lots of fun.
But when we ask about her mask—
She isn't wearing one.

So if you're in our neighborhood,
Be sure to come our way.
We've got some candy just for you
That's ten years old today.

Love Song of a Werewolf

By Jennifer Cole Judd

The black night is perfect,
The moon, cold and sallow.
The trees sway in shadows,
The goblin winds moan.

I race and I rage
With no creature to stop me.
I'm fierce and I'm fearless,
Yet I am alone.

Alone and so lonely,
My ragged howl echoes—
A mournful, lost cry
In a damp, dreary cave.

But you! You would make
This night so inviting,
The hunt more exciting.
Come with me—be brave.

Though some flee before me,
I'm really quite charming.
I'm sweet as a puppy—
Romantic, polite.

Come with me, my love,
And we'll chase down the moonlight.
You've nothing to fear.
I will take
    Just
        One
           Bite!

Spooky Jack

By Jennifer Cole Judd

On Halloween, I saw a sign:
"Come pick a pumpkin from the vine!"
I spied a plump one in the back,
And knew he'd be my "Spooky Jack."

I took him home and grabbed a knife
To make my pumpkin come to life.
I carved out eyes, a ghoulish grin,
Then put a burning candle in.

I stood up to inspect my work.
He glowered with a creepy smirk.
And now I want to put him back,
'Cause he just cackled, "Come to JACK!"

The Witching Hour

By Angela McMullen

On moonless nights she lies in bed,
With sleepless eyelids twitching.
Her breathing stops, the clock *tick-tocks*—
The hour of the Witching.

While shadows tiptoe through the room,
Her prickling scalp gives warning.
She pulls the sheets above her head
And wishes it were morning.

As jet-black figures fiercely growl
And wind their way upstairs,
She squeezes shut her weary eyes
And whispers desperate prayers.

When scratching fingers reach the door,
She starts to gasp and shake.
She feels her heart pound *thump, thump, thump,*
And waits for day to break.

At last when brilliant sun spills in
And floods her room with light,
She's thankful that she's once again
Survived a Witching night.

The Goblin Parade

By Jennifer Cole Judd

When the silvery moon
Glimmers out from the gloom
On the blackest of black Halloweens,
While the children are sleeping
The shadows come creeping,
To begin the most frightening of scenes.

With a *rum-tilly-tum*,
The low beat of a drum
Ushers in quite a bone-chilling sight,
As above howling winds,
The music begins—
The goblin parade is tonight!

In the inky black street
Their fat, knobbly feet
Stomp a rhythm that makes the earth shake.
They gallop through town,
Tearing tree branches down.
They are hungry for mischief to make.

They're slashing their claws,
And they're chomping their jaws
On mailboxes, streetlamps, and cars.
They charge through the park,
Climb on roofs in the dark,
And gleefully screech at the stars.

Their stubby gray snouts
Snuffle-sniff all about—
They have found what they like best to eat.
Not a snake, nor a mouse,
No—they're eyeing *your* house,
For *you* are their favorite treat!

Haunted

By William Shakespeery

Gaunt and ghastly, Greta Lynn
Is scarcely bone with paper skin.
Her breath is stale and cold as snow,
And when she walks, the ravens crow.

Poor Greta was a lonely child—
She had no friends, she never smiled.
In school I called her shameful things—
I shouted cruel and painful things.

Now every night at twelve o'clock,
I hear her shuffling up the block.
And every night, she tries my lock,
Then gives my door a hollow knock.

She calls my name, then thumps the wall.
My bedroom quakes and pictures fall.
I close my eyes and plug my ears,
For she's been dead for seven years.

October 31st

By William Shakespeery

"I'll grease my hair," said Frankenstein,
"And comb a little curl.
Tonight I'm going trick-or-treating
As a flower girl."

"That curls my blood," the vampire hissed.
"You might make someone faint.
I bought a gown and miter hat;
I'm going as a saint."

The werewolf barked, "I've got a cap,
And boots to hide my paws.
My mama sewed a big red coat
To make me Santa Claus."

"That's truly chilling," cried the witch.
"That's such a spooky creature.
But I think I can top you all;
I'm going as a teacher."

"Oh, jeepers creepers!" gasped the troll.
"If I could go, I would.
It's just my parents say it's wrong
To make believe you're good."

The Highland Train

By Laura Wynkoop

One hundred years ago tonight,
When clouds obscured the heavens' light,
The track was slick and silver-white
Along this cold plateau.

The Highland Train was running late.
The track curved west; the train went straight.
On screaming brakes, it met its fate
Beneath the falling snow.

Now once a year, you hear *click-clack*,
And catch a glimpse of gleaming black.
The Highland's ghost sweeps down the track,
Its windowpanes aglow.

The engine's haunting yellow eye
Illuminates those passing by,
While hissing steam fades in the sky,
And coal-fire burns below.

Its whistle echoes low and clear,
But then the train will disappear.
And moaning wind is all you'll hear
Along this cold plateau.

The Scarecrow

By Angela McMullen

In tattered rags he stands and waits
Against his gnarled post.
The blue dawn steals across his face
As swiftly as a ghost.

The wind wraps 'round the silent man
And stirs his stringy hair.
The cornstalks shiver in the breeze,
Awakened by his stare.

Crows avoid the tempting field,
Their black eyes bright with fear.
They gather speed as they fly past,
Afraid to go too near.

With face fixed in a jagged grin,
His body shifts and yields
As gusts of wind dance back and forth
Across the lonely fields.

Swamp Witch

By Susie Sawyer

Where peepers peep,
And creepers creep,
Where dead, decaying things rot deep
Beneath the murky muck and mud,
She lurks and lives alone.

With wicked grin,
And fingers thin,
Her carcass draped with slimy skin,
The echo of her shrieking howl
Will chill you to the bone.

She seeks a soul
To make her whole,
So best beware of where you stroll.
For if you wander in too close,
She'll steal yours for her own.

The Giant's Pocket

By M. Sullivan

I'm stuck inside the pocket
Of a giant, dreadful beast—
A brute who stomps upon the earth,
Whose footsteps never cease.
All I feel is motion.
I can't see moon or sun.
I'm rolled about like nickels
When he begins to run.

I don't remember food.
I don't remember drink.
I don't remember many things,
And now I need to think,
Of who I am and where I am,
And how I came to be
Inside this giant's pocket,
And how
I might
   Slip
      Free.

The Gargoyle

By Kevin McNamee

High above the bustling street,
I sit alone both day and night.
My talons, horns, and outstretched wings
Create a ghastly, gruesome sight.

But if you look at me, you'll see,
I am not all that I appear.
Come close, for I have tales to tell.
I've many stories you should hear.

But where shall I begin my tales?
I've seen much from this lonely post.
Come closer; look me in the eyes,
And hear what you
should fear the most.

Too late! I've cast my
spell on you!
Now you're a gargoyle
just like me;
For those who gaze
into my eyes
Are doomed to keep
me company.

The Wishing Well

By Laura Wynkoop

Throughout the dark and creeping woods, there lies a hidden trail
That wanders to a wishing well within a misty vale.

The local townsfolk, young and old, all know the well is cursed,
And those who dare to make a wish had best expect the worst.

But still each year, unheeding children close their eyes and grin.
They focus on their deepest dreams and throw their pennies in.

Before their pennies plunge too far, those children hear the sound
Of grumbling growls and scraping claws from deep beneath the ground.

A slimy, withered hand appears with skin a ghostly gray.
The children freeze—they barely breathe, too scared to run away.

An eyeless beast with jagged teeth soon clambers from the well
To search for frightened children with its heightened sense of smell.

From time to time, brave children find the strength to turn around;
They race along the trail and make it safely back to town.

But those remaining, stiff from fear, will face the beast's attack.
They'll disappear into the well—those children won't come back.

So if you ever chance upon that well within the vale,
I pray you'll stop and think about this cautionary tale.

If fear beyond your wildest dreams is what you seek within,
Then by all means, just go ahead,
And throw your penny in.

A Monster in My Bathroom

By Christy Critchfield

There's a monster in my bathroom,
Something hideous and vile.
As I enter, I am frightened
By its crooked, drooling smile.

My heart—it stops.
My breath—it quickens.
The tension in the room—
It thickens.
The air is cold, the lights are dim.
He looks at me, I look at him.

With crusty eyes, a vacant stare,
Mangy, matted, messy hair,
A puffy face and scruffy chin,
Zit-infested, pallid skin,
Teeth encased in grime and gunk,
Breath that smells of rotting skunk.

Despite near paralyzing fright
From such a nasty, wretched sight,
I bravely take a few steps nearer,
Where things become a whole lot clearer. . . .

I am looking in a mirror.

Coming Home from Trick-or-Treating

By Jennifer Cole Judd

Did I just hear a whispering
Behind those swaying trees?
Was that a thud beyond that gate,
Or just my knocking knees?

Is that a shadow of a cat
Beside that garden shed?
Or could it be a zombie who's
Forgotten that he's dead?

There's nothing to be scared of now.
Tonight is just for fun.
Except . . . what's that? A vampire bat?
Excuse me, gotta run!

Read at Your Own Risk

By Christy Critchfield

For all who bravely dare
To read this haunted sonnet,
May you be made aware
A spell's been cast upon it.

Proceed to read this rhyme.
You'll be in lots of trouble.
Your skin will turn to slime
And slowly start to bubble.

You'll quickly shrink in size,
Then grow a little greenish,
Acquire a taste for flies
(I hope you're not too squeamish!).

Your only hope to avoid this fate?
Don't read the ending. . . . Oops, too late!

(Ribbit . . . Ribbit . . .)